For Spotty, Hawkeye, and Coach—the three dogs in my life,
who have shared their love, understanding, and joy
Love, L.M.

For Ed and Mie, my fantastic parents —S.V.D.

Text copyright © 2013 by Lisa Moser
Jacket art and interior illustrations copyright © 2013 by Sebastiaan Van Doninck

Visit us on the Web!
randomhouse.com/kids

Educators and librarians, for a variety of teaching tools, visit us at
RHTeachersLibrarians.com

Library of Congress Cataloging-in-Publication Data
Moser, Lisa.
Cowboy Boyd and Mighty Calliope / by Lisa Moser ; illustrated by Sebastiaan Van Doninck. — 1st ed.
p. cm.
Summary: A cowboy and his trusty rhinoceros try to prove themselves at the Double R Ranch, where Slim, Hardtack, and Rancher Rose doubt Calliope's potential, but Boyd believes in her.
ISBN 978-0-375-87056-9 (trade) — ISBN 978-0-375-97056-6 (lib. bdg.) — ISBN 978-0-375-98079-4 (ebook)
[1. Cowboys—Fiction. 2. Rhinoceroses—Fiction. 3. Ranch life—Fiction.] I. Doninck, Sebastiaan Van, ill. II. Title.
PZ7.M84696Cow 2013 [Fic]—dc23 2012025379

MANUFACTURED IN CHINA
10 9 8 7 6 5 4 3 2 1
First Edition
Random House Children's Books supports the First Amendment and celebrates the right to read.

Cowboy Boyd and Mighty Calliope

and

by Lisa Moser

illustrated by Sebastiaan Van Doninck

Random House New York

No doubt about it, folks knew Boyd and Calliope
were different the moment they rode onto the Double R Ranch.

"That's the shortest horse I've ever seen," said Slim.

"That's the dustiest horse I've ever seen," said Hardtack.

"That's the lumpiest horse I've ever seen," said Rancher Rose.

"She's a rare one," said Boyd. "Raised her myself."

He patted Calliope's thick hide and slid out of the saddle.
"We're looking for a place to call home. We'd be mighty obliged
if you let us work on your ranch."

"I suppose we could try it," said Rancher Rose, eyeing Calliope.

"You won't regret it," said Boyd. "I got a real strong belief
in Calliope."

Fence mending was the first chore. Calliope did
a good job hauling fence posts.

KER-THUD, KER-THUD, KER-THUD.

But it took a long time.

"I call that real talent," said Boyd.

"I call that real unusual," said Slim.

"I call that real slow," said Hardtack.

"Calliope's not a sprinter. She's more of a plodder," said Boyd, rubbing her dusty nose. "But she's real steady."

Rancher Rose shook her head.

"We moved the cattle to the north pasture,"
said Rancher Rose. "You and Calliope ride out on
the range and bring home any strays you find."

"Count on us!" said Boyd, plodding off on Calliope.
KER-THUD, KER-THUD, KER-THUD.

"We found some strays," said Boyd. Calliope wagged her tail.

"That's a prairie dog," said Hardtack.

"That's a jackrabbit," said Slim.

"That's a coyote!" said Rancher Rose.

"They were drawn to Calliope's natural friendliness,"
said Boyd, giving Calliope a hug. "Like chicks to a hen."
Rancher Rose shook her head. She pumped fresh water
into the trough. "You two show Boyd where to bunk. I'll finish here."

When the horses and Calliope finished drinking,
Rancher Rose opened the pasture gate. "Off to bed," she said.
KER-THUD, KER-THUD, KER-THUD.
Calliope plodded to the pasture and . . .

BLAM! Straight through the pasture fence.

BLAM! Straight through the barn wall.

BLAM! Straight through the bunkhouse door.

"She just doesn't know her own strength," said Boyd, tucking Calliope in.

Rancher Rose shook her head.

Boyd followed Rancher Rose out to the campfire.
"I'm real sorry," said Rancher Rose, twiddling her hat,
"but Calliope is not working out."

Boyd stared at the fire and sighed. "That's a shame. Thing is, I think Calliope would have really surprised you." He stood up and shook Rancher Rose's hand. "We'll head out in the morning," said Boyd, "but we sure enjoyed working here, even for a short bit."

That night, a storm hammered the Double R Ranch.
Thunder cracked and rain poured in buckets.

Hours later, just when the bunkhouse had settled back to sleep, the door flew open.

"The cattle are gone!" yelled Rancher Rose. "Slim! Hardtack! Saddle up!"

Everyone rushed out.

Boyd stroked Calliope's face. "This is a dire situation," he said.
"But I got a real strong belief in you."

Calliope nuzzled Boyd while he pulled on his boots.

When Boyd and Calliope caught up, the cowboys looked
worried and their horses were blowing hard.

"I've never seen the cattle so skittish," said Rancher Rose.
"Every time we race in, they scatter like tumbleweed in a
windstorm. If we don't round them up soon, they'll stampede."

"Mind if Calliope and I try?" asked Boyd.

"Calliope's too slow," said Slim.

"Calliope's too clumsy," said Hardtack.

"Calliope's just what we need," said Boyd, smiling.

KER-THUD, KER-THUD, KER-THUD.
Calliope plodded into the field—slow and steady.
She went up to a baby calf and wagged her tail. She plodded
a few steps and looked back.

The baby followed.
Its mama followed.
The whole, entire herd followed.
Like chicks to a hen.

Calliope led them all the way home.
BLAM! Straight through the prickly bushes.

BLAM! Straight through the tangled briars.

BLAM! Straight through the bunkhouse door.

"You're some kind of animal," said Slim.

"You're some kind of cowboy," said Hardtack.

"You're Cowboy Boyd and Mighty Calliope," said Rancher Rose, "and we'd be mighty obliged if you made your home on the Double R Ranch. We got a real strong belief in you."

Cowboy Boyd hollered, "Yip-yip-yippee!"
Everyone cheered!

Mighty Calliope rolled in the dirt.